Bungee Hero

by

Julie Bertagna

Illustrated by Martin Salisbury

You do not need to read this page –
ju~~st get on with~~ the book!

First published 1999 in Great Britain by
Barrington Stoke Ltd
10 Belford Terrace, Edinburgh, EH4 3DQ
Reprinted 1999, 2000

This edition first published 2001
Reprinted 2001

ISBN 1-902260-91-0
Previously published by Barrington Stoke Ltd under ISBN 1-902260-23-6

Printed by Polestar AUP Aberdeen Ltd

Meet The Author - Julie Bertagna

What is your favourite animal?
A tiger

What is your favourite boy's name?
Michael

What is your favourite girl's name?
Natalie

What is your favourite food?
Peking Duck with Chinese
Pancakes

What is your favourite music?
Loud and lots of it!

What is your favourite hobby?
Buying too many CDs

Meet The Illustrator - Martin Salisbury

What is your favourite animal?
Any wild cat

What is your favourite boy's name?
Charles

What is your favourite girl's name?
Stella

What is your favourite food?
Sausages and mash

What is your favourite music?
Patsy Cline

What is your favourite hobby?
Collecting illustrated books

For heroic moments
And to Sandra, for the idea

Contents

Chapter 1
Adam Meets a Grumpy Hero

Adam slammed an amazing shot past the goalie. Yes! It was in! The huge crowd rose to its feet and roared. Adam raised his fists in a victory salute. He was a hero. He would go down in history as a football legend. He was Adam Moffat, striker of the century.

"Hurry up and get in the car, Adam."

"Aw, Mum," groaned Adam. "Do I have to?"

The imaginary football crowd vanished along with the teams. The massive football ground inside Adam's head melted away too and he was back in his own garden. He took one last shot at his imaginary football, pretending to smash it through the living-room window, and got in the car.

Mum gave him a long look. "You'll pay for that out of your pocket money," she told him, with a perfectly straight face.

Adam laughed. Mum might be a pain in the neck about some things but she could take a joke.

"Do we have to go to that stupid old people's nursing home today?" Adam moaned. "Everybody else goes down to the burger bar after school on a Friday."

"They can manage without you for an hour," Mum replied. "Anyway, I only need you to shift a few boxes. It'll be good exercise. Surely a football hero needs to be fit."

"Not an imaginary one," Adam muttered as they drove off to the nursing home. "I just imagine I'm fit."

Adam's Mum was a helper at the old people's nursing home. Sometimes, she asked Adam to come along and help out.

Mum loved listening to the old people's life stories. They bored Adam out of his mind. Especially on a Friday after school, when he should have been down at the burger bar, planning out the weekend with Micko and Gary.

"Did I tell you old Mrs Carey was once a cancan dancer?" said Mum. "She wore a sparkly leotard and pink feathers in her hair. Hard to believe, isn't it?"

Not *hard* to believe, thought Adam. Impossible. He didn't care if Mrs Carey had once been a lion tamer. It was so long ago it was ancient history. Now she was just another boring old wrinkly, like all the rest.

Adam went down to the stock room in the nursing home's basement and began to shift boxes of tinned food up to the kitchen. It seemed to take ages and Mum still wasn't ready when he had finished.

"Another ten minutes won't kill you, Adam," she told him. "I just want to take Mr Haddock out for a bit of fresh air. He's been in bed all week with a nasty cold."

Adam looked at his watch. Another ten minutes *might* kill him. He might die of boredom. Micko and Gary would be off somewhere without him if he didn't get down to the burger bar soon.

While Mum collected Mr Haddock, Adam passed the time in imagining the old man as a large fish in a wheelchair. An old wrinkled haddock who told long, boring tales about his long, boring life swimming round and round a boring sea.

But Mr Haddock turned out to be just an ordinary old man in a wheelchair. Mind you, his eyes were a bit fishy-looking, thought Adam. He began to dribble his imaginary football back and forth in front of the wheelchair as Mum pushed Mr Haddock around the nursing home grounds.

"Adam!" hissed Mum, as he sliced a shot over the old man's head. He was pretending Mr Haddock was an attacking midfielder – a pretty slow one, it had to be said.

Mr Haddock looked at Adam with fierce, unfriendly blue eyes.

"I dare say *I'd* rather play invisible football than trail about with a useless old fogey in a wheelchair," Mr Haddock said.

The football game in Adam's head cut dead. Mum glared angrily at him. Adam followed quietly behind Mum and Mr Haddock for the

rest of the walk. He didn't want to risk losing his burger money.

"Mr Haddock was a parachutist in the Second World War, Adam," said Mum, as they circled back round to the nursing home. "He was awarded a medal for bravery."

"So what?" Adam muttered. He checked his watch. Micko and Gary would have given up on him by now. The last thing he needed was this old croaky to start nattering on about the Second World War.

But the old man just looked over the gardens with his fierce eyes.

"That's exactly what I think," Mr Haddock said, after a moment. "So what?"

Adam caught his breath. He'd thought the old man was too deaf to hear what he had said.

Mum looked furious now.

"You'll have to excuse Adam, Mr Haddock," she said. "He's impatient to get out with his friends. And he's hungry. That's what's making him so rude."

"Ah," said Mr Haddock, giving Adam another sharp look. "I see."

"Bye," murmured Adam, as Mum pushed the old man up the wheelchair ramp at the nursing home entrance. Mr Haddock didn't so much as glance at him.

Funny, thought Adam, but Mr Haddock really did look a bit like a fish. He had a long, glum face with a downturned mouth and those fierce staring eyes. Maybe there was a fish tail instead of legs under the thick tartan rug that was tucked around his lower body. Adam laughed to himself and glanced back at the old man.

A jolt of shock hit Adam as he looked closer. The tartan rug lay flat against the leg rest of the wheelchair. The foot rest was empty too.

Mr Haddock could never have been a parachutist in the Second World War, thought Adam. It wasn't possible.

The old man had no legs.

Chapter 2
Mr Vertigo

"Are you sure Mr Haddock's not just spinning a story about being a war hero?" Adam asked on the way home. "Remember that old lady who told you all about her twenty-six grandchildren. Then you found out she never had a family. She'd just imagined it all!"

Mum shook her head.

"Mr Haddock's all there. He hasn't always been an old man in a wheelchair, Adam. There are some faded photographs in his room. One is of a boy about your age, with a football at his feet. I'm sure it's him. The other is of a young man making a parachute landing. I'm sure that's him too. He was very handsome."

Adam found it impossible to imagine the fierce old man in the wheelchair as either a boy playing football *or* a handsome young parachutist.

"How did he lose his legs?" he asked.

"I don't know," said Mum. "It's not really something you ask, is it?"

Mum stopped the car outside the burger bar. Micko and Gary were at the usual window seat where they could ogle and stare at passing girls.

"See, they haven't deserted you," said Mum. "There was no need for all that rudeness with Mr Haddock."

"Sorry," said Adam, sheepishly. He gave Mum his sweetest smile. "I lifted all those boxes," he reminded her.

"You did," she laughed, handing him his burger money. "But next time have a little more respect for an old man who risked his life for you."

For me? thought Adam, as he queued for his burger and coke. Nothing to do with me. I wasn't even born.

Yet, as he waited in the long queue, Adam began to wonder what it was like being a war hero, parachuting down into enemy territory on a dangerous mission.

"Where've you been?" said Micko, when Adam finally joined them. "The carnival's down at the waterfront. Get a move on with that burger and we'll head down there."

Gary grinned. "Mr Vertigo's Big Wheel is gi-normous. The biggest in Europe. You can see it from my bedroom window."

Adam gulped down the last of his burger.

"Excellent. Let's go!"

*****

The carnival was right beside the river that ran through the heart of the city. As darkness fell the waterfront began to teem with noise and colour and movement. The brilliant glitter of the carnival's lights scattered all across the river.

By the time Adam and his friends got there the carnival was in full swing. They headed straight for Mr Vertigo's Big Wheel. It *was* gi-normous, thought Adam. His heart thudded in his chest as he looked up at the carriages that spun high into the night sky.

People piled off Mr Vertigo's Big Wheel, still laughing and screaming. Suddenly Adam realised he didn't want to go on. He was too scared. Terrified, in fact. Yet if he chickened out, Micko and Gary would pester him about it for the rest of his life. He *had* to go on.

As he locked the safety bar across his seat, Adam wished he was anywhere else in the

world. The swaying, jerking carriage lifted him higher and higher into the darkness. Adam was terrified.

At the top of Mr Vertigo's Big Wheel Adam could hardly bear it. He was even higher than the huge, dockyard crane that sat on the opposite riverbank. He could see to the very edges of the city where the lights scattered into blackness. The gleaming trail of the river ran for miles. Adam was so high he felt he could almost reach out and touch a star – except he couldn't let go of the safety bar.

He was so high he felt sick.

Adam closed his eyes as Mr Vertigo jerked into action and the carriage bucked wildly up and down. There was an instant when he seemed to dangle helplessly in space. Then he plunged downwards, fast and hard. Wind blasted in his face and he screamed.

The carriage tipped forwards and when Adam opened his eyes he was hurtling towards the ground. He was going to smash to earth!

At that instant the carriage jerked back upwards as Mr Vertigo spun him skywards once more. Adam had a moment of relief – until he realised he would have to do it all again.

And again, and again, until Mr Vertigo decided to stop.

By the time Adam got off Mr Vertigo he felt as if his arms and legs had been blasted to the corners of the sky then stuck back on again in any old order. Only his thumping heart had stayed put through the terrifying ride.

Yet deep inside, beyond the sickening terror, there was a thrilling, crackling excitement.

"I did it!" Adam laughed, as he raced to the Dodgems with Micko and Gary. "I really did it!"

All of a sudden he thought of Mr Haddock, but not as a fierce old man in a wheelchair. Instead, Adam saw him as a young parachutist, dropping out of the sky, plunging through darkness and crashing to earth.

Adam wondered if Mr Haddock had felt the same strange mix of thrill and terror that he had felt as he tumbled through the sky on Mr Vertigo's Big Wheel.

Chapter 3
The War Diary

Adam thought about Mr Haddock all week. He wasn't sure why, but as the week went on he played less and less invisible football. Instead, Adam began to imagine himself as a Second World War parachutist, dropping into enemy territory on a secret mission.

"You don't need to come with me to the nursing home today, Adam," Mum told him on

Friday afternoon. "Off you go and enjoy yourself."

"Oh," said Adam.

Mum looked at him. "What's wrong?"

"Nothing," said Adam. "I just thought I'd maybe take Mr Haddock out for a walk."

"Mr Haddock!" cried Mum. "Why on earth? You didn't exactly hit it off with him last week."

"What do you mean?" muttered Adam.

"Oh come on, Adam," said Mum. "What are you up to?"

"Nothing," Adam bluffed. "It's just that we're doing the Second World War in school and I wanted to ask him something."

"Oh, homework," nodded Mum. "Why didn't you say so? Well, make sure you're polite to him this time."

"I'll be an angel," grinned Adam.

*****

Mr Haddock wasn't in the mood for visiting angels, or anyone else.

"What's this?" he grumbled, when Adam knocked on his door and asked if he'd like some fresh air. "Has your mother given you extra pocket money to visit me, eh?"

"No," muttered Adam.

Once again, it was impossible to imagine this grumpy old man as a brave young war hero.

Adam was glad to get behind the wheelchair where he could escape Mr Haddock's fierce stare. He pushed the old man through the nursing home grounds, wondering why on earth he had bothered to come.

"Now why would a young lad like you want to push an old grump around when you could be off with your friends?" Mr Haddock demanded all of a sudden, as if he had just read Adam's mind.

"I – I don't know," said Adam. "I just – I wanted to ask you about the war."

"Ah," said Mr Haddock. "Schoolwork, is it?"

"Yes ... I mean no ... I mean," Adam sighed. What *was* it he wanted to ask? "You see, I was on Mr Vertigo's Big Wheel the other day, at the carnival. It was so ..."

Adam stopped. He was embarrassed to admit to a war hero that it had been terrifying.

"It was amazing," Adam continued. "Really wild. And I thought it must be a bit like a parachute jump."

"So you want to know what it's like doing a parachute jump, eh?" barked Mr Haddock. "Well, I've never been on a Big Wheel but getting ready to jump from a plane drop hole as you fly over enemy territory is like getting ready to jump into hell. It's no carnival ride, that I can tell you. You don't risk your life on a Big Wheel, do you, boy?"

"No," said Adam, through gritted teeth.

The old man was a real horror. Adam turned the wheelchair around and pushed back towards the nursing home. He parked Mr Haddock in front of the TV without another

word and went to wait by the car for his
mother.

He should never have come. It had been a
complete waste of time.

*****

On Monday morning a parcel arrived in the post for Adam.

"Who's sending you presents?" asked his Dad.

"Don't know," said Adam as he tore it open. Inside was a brown leather notebook. PLEASE RETURN IN GOOD CONDITION TO E. HADDOCK, said a notelet stuck on the front.

Adam looked inside. The pages had yellowed with age and were covered in small, cramped writing, as if the writer had been scared of running out of space. A small dust cloud gathered as he flicked through the pages.

"Adam!" Mum flapped her hand in front of her face. "Hey, I'm getting dust in my cornflakes."

Adam stopped at a random page and read:

May 17th 1944. 22.20 hours

Just about to leave on my third sortie to fly over occupied France. It's another mission to map out the position of enemy troops in the north. But this is the most dangerous yet. Jack reckons the odd bit of sniper gunfire we've had to dodge so far will be nothing compared to the anti-aircraft gunners we expect tonight. A last cuppa then we're off.

*****

10.00 hours

Back in one piece! Could kill for a bacon butty.

*****

Below this, the words were scrawled and hard to read:

Jack's plane didn't make it back.
My best buddy. I feel he's going to
walk in the door any minute, yelling
for his bacon butty. Will he?

*****

"Time for school, Adam, and you've hardly eaten a mouthful," said Mum.

"What's this wonderful book then?" asked Dad. "It must be something special if it's keeping you off breakfast."

Adam felt dazed.

"It's from Mr Haddock," he said. "He's sent me his war diary."

Chapter 4
Drop Zone Disaster

Adam shoved Mr Haddock's war diary in his schoolbag but it was break-time before he got a chance to look at it again. In the playground he flicked through the dusty pages, trying to find the bit he had read at breakfast.

What had happened to Jack, Mr Haddock's best buddy? Did he get back safely? Was his plane shot down? Adam hadn't been able to think of anything else all morning.

Mr Haddock's cramped handwriting was hard to read, and Adam couldn't remember the date of the diary entries he had looked at before. When the bell rang at the end of break, Adam still hadn't found out what had happened to Jack.

It took Adam half of his lunch-break to find the right place. Then, at last, he found the answer. Jack's plane *had* been shot down over France by anti-aircraft gunners. He never came back. Mr Haddock lost his best buddy.

Adam stood in the school playground staring into space.

Micko thumped him on the shoulder. "What planet are you on?"

"Look," said Adam. He showed Micko the war diary and told him all about it.

Micko blew out a sigh as he examined the book.

"One day you're best mates and the next day one of you is dead. What a weird thought," Micko said.

The two boys looked at each other for a moment as the awfulness of it sunk in. Suddenly, Adam wasn't sure if he wanted to read any more of the diary. He enjoyed playing war games on his computer but Mr Haddock's diary wasn't a game. It was real. That made it almost too painful to read.

All the same, Adam took the diary up to his
room after dinner that evening. He started to
read it from the beginning.

He read about the tough training
programme Mr Haddock had to complete to
become a parachutist, and about his night-time
sorties flying over France. Once again he read
about Jack's death.

It seemed Mr Haddock hardly had time to
take in his friend's death before he was off on a
special mission. His most dangerous mission
yet.

*****

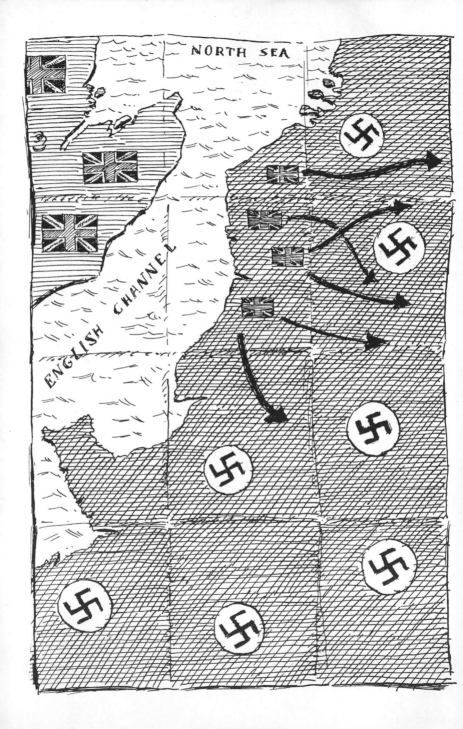

May 24th 1944

   *"You don't get to be a war hero because
you kill the enemy," our mission leader said
tonight. "And being scared doesn't make
you a coward. It's giving freedom to another
human being that makes you a hero."*

   *But I don't want to be a hero any more.
I thought I did. Both Jack and I did. Now
he's dead and tonight I'd give anything
just to be back in my old, ordinary life,
playing a game of football with my best
buddy. Yet the lives of so many people
depend on this mission. Hitler's armies
are on the move across France and
we must help the Resistance forces in
their fight against them.*

   *Tonight I must parachute into enemy
territory. I've only ever done practice jumps
before but I've imagined the real thing so
many times.*

The plane lights will switch off as we reach our drop zone. I will take my place and get ready to jump from the plane's drop hole. Below me will be black, empty space. When we spot the signal – a single beam of torchlight in a field – I must jump. I'll tip forward and fall into thin air. I can only pray that no enemy gunners lie in wait and that it's a safe landing.

I'm sick with terror. But I must do it. The mission must succeed. I will do it for Jack.

*****

The next page was blank. It seemed to be the end of the diary. Then Adam found one more entry a few pages on.

November 1945

The war is now over. And today I found this old diary again. I could hardly bear to read it. This will be my last entry, though I don't know why I write it. Who will ever read this diary but me?

That night of the mission we flew over the drop zone but there was no torch signal. They have forgotten, we thought. We didn't want to think they had been taken prisoner, or killed. But I had important intelligence information to give to the Resistance. I had to make the jump.

I will never forget the moment I tipped out of the plane drop hole. It was sheer terror! Freezing wind blasted me as I plunged through the darkness. There was a great jolt as my parachute opened. Then there was the most amazing feeling, a hot rush of fire that burned through my terror.

It was the feeling of being truly alive. *I did it!* I told myself as I crashed to earth.

But I hadn't – not yet. A moment later the world exploded in my face.

This wasn't the drop zone. It was the wrong field. I had landed upon a minefield.

I don't remember anything else until the day I woke up in terrible pain in a strange bed. They told me I'd lost my legs in the blast. At that moment I wished I was dead. I had failed. I was no hero.

But they told me I was a hero. The intelligence reports I had strapped to my chest in a special wallet survived the blast. The Resistance forces had used them to save many lives. All those lives must be worth the sacrifice of one man's legs.

To win freedom for others, I had to lose my own.

*****

Adam closed the diary. He felt very strange. But then the most amazing idea gripped him.

Adam knew the amazing idea was meant for him. He wasn't sure why, but it felt like his mission. A very special mission. The mission of his life.

Chapter 5
Mission Bungee

"A parachute jump?" said Micko. "Are you off your head?"

Micko and Gary stared at Adam in amazement.

"How can you do a parachute jump when you nearly chickened out of the Big Wheel?" said Gary. "You were totally chicken. I saw you."

"I was not!" Adam lied. "And I never chickened out, did I?"

"How do you get to do a parachute jump?" asked Micko.

"Haven't a clue," Adam admitted. "Any ideas?"

Gary looked blank.

Micko shrugged.

"Look it up in the Yellow Pages?" said Adam.

*****

The first flying school Adam phoned almost put a stop to the special mission before it had even begun.

"Sorry, son. You've got to be over sixteen to do a parachute jump," the instructor told him.

Adam groaned.

"Mission cancelled," he told the others.

"Special mission, is it?" asked the voice on the phone. "Does it have to be a parachute jump?"

"Yeah," said Adam.

"Pity," said the instructor, "because there's always bungee jumping. That's as close as you can get."

"A bungee jump!" yelled Adam. He let the phone drop in excitement. "That'll do. I'll make it Mission Bungee!"

*****

"Your mother will go ⌐
father, when he hea⌐
"Forget it, Adam."

"But it's in a good cau⌐

"It's in a very good cause.
the idea of it and neither will y⌐
said his Dad.

Adam's Mum didn't go bananas. Sh⌐
said no, absolutely not.

Adam was about to bang the living-room
door behind him and storm upstairs when he
thought of something better. He brought out Mr
Haddock's war diary.

"Listen to this," he pleaded.

He read the bit about Jack and the entry
written the night before Mr Haddock's
parachute jump. Then he read the last entry of
all.

ars in a wheelchair," said Dad at
here must be so many other young
lost their freedom like Mr Haddock
t the rest of their lives in hospitals
sing homes for the war wounded."

breaks your heart," said Mum. "But I don't
hat's to be gained by Adam risking his life
bungee jump."

"I'm not risking my life," Adam argued. "I'll
ave a safety harness and helmet and there'll
be bungee experts there to make sure
everything's OK."

"But why?" Mum demanded.

"I want to do a sponsored jump," explained
Adam, "to raise money for an electric
wheelchair. You said Mr Haddock hadn't the
strength to wheel himself about any more. It'll
give him a bit of freedom. He deserves that,
doesn't he, after what he did?"

58

Adam also remembered the words in Mr Haddock's diary. The thrill and terror of the parachute jump was the feeling of being truly alive, Mr Haddock had written.

"I really want to do it," Adam told his parents.

"All right," said Mum at last. "If you can prove to me it's safe, you can do it. But don't come crying to me if you break your neck!"

*****

"Ready?" asked the bungee instructor.

Adam panicked. He would never be ready. This was a mad idea – a very bad, mad idea. He no longer cared if he chickened out and made a fool of himself in front of Mum and Dad, Micko and Gary, the newspaper reporters, and all the kids and teachers from school. He was too terrified to care. He just could not do it.

Mission Bungee had become quite an event. "Do it somewhere unexpected," the instructor had said, "then you'll get a big crowd. The more people you get, the more money you'll raise." For some reason Adam had thought of the huge dockyard crane on the waterfront, the one he had seen from the top of the Big Wheel that night at the carnival. The bungee instructors had checked it out and said it was perfect.

Now he was standing on top of the dockyard crane in front of a huge crowd, getting ready to do a bungee jump.

Adam looked across at the Big Wheel on the other side of the river. It sat still and colourless in the daylight. Mr Haddock was right. A ride on Mr Vertigo was a joke compared to this. Yet even a bungee jump couldn't be as scary as a real parachute jump. One that landed you in enemy territory in the dead of night, right on top of an exploding landmine.

You didn't even hit the ground in a bungee jump. You just landed upside down in mid-air attached to an elastic safety rope.

I'll die of fright, thought Adam.

Then he spotted Mr Haddock in his wheelchair, beside Mum and Dad. When he had told Mr Haddock about the bungee jump and why he was doing it, the old man had looked at him in disbelief then his fierce eyes had filled with tears. They'd had a long talk that afternoon, he and Mr Haddock.

Now as Adam looked down, the old man touched his forehead in a salute.

Adam let out a great breath. He could chicken out in front of everyone else but somehow he could not let Mr Haddock down.

What was it Mr Haddock's mission leader had said in the war diary? Being scared doesn't make you a coward. But giving freedom to another human being makes you a hero.

Adam closed his eyes. He counted three loud, thudding heartbeats. He tipped forwards.

Then he let himself fall.

Who is Barrington Stoke?

Barrington Stoke was a famous and much-loved story-teller. He travelled from village to village carrying a lantern to light his way. He arrived as it grew dark and when the young boys and girls of the village saw the glow of his lantern, they hurried to the central meeting place. They were full of excitement and expectation, for his stories were always wonderful.

Then Barrington Stoke set down his lantern. In the flickering light the listeners were enthralled by his tales of adventure, horror and mystery. He knew exactly what they liked best and he loved telling a good story. And another. And then another. When the lantern burned low and dawn was nearly breaking, he slipped away. He was gone by morning, only to appear the next day in some other village to tell the next story.

If you loved this story, why don't you read ...

Ship of Ghosts

by Nigel Hinton

Have you sometimes longed for excitement and adventure? Mick has wanted to go to sea ever since he learned that his Dad was a sailor. His dreams come true. But what he discovers on the Ship of Ghosts turn his dreams into a nightmare.

You can order this book directly from Macmillan Distribution Ltd, Brunel Road, Houndmills, Basingstoke, Hampshire RG21 6XS   Tel: 01256 302699